To Sir John Templeton

For a legacy of supporting the
principles of peace and prosperity.

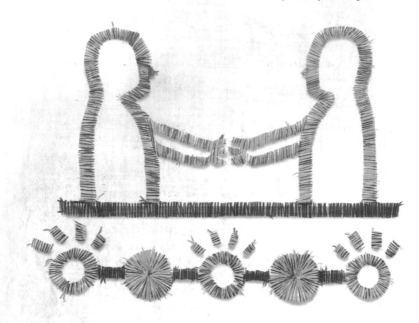

No graphic, visual, electronic, film, microfilm, tape recording, or any other means may be
used to reproduce in any form, without prior written permission of the author, except in the
case of brief passages embodied in critical reviews and articles.

ISBN 978-1-943521-17-3

Boyack, Connor, author.
Stanfield, Elijah, illustrator.
The Tuttle Twins and the Golden Rule / Connor Boyack.

Cover design by Elijah Stanfield
Edited and typeset by Connor Boyack

Printed in the United States

THE TUTTLE TWINS
and the
GOLDEN RULE

CONNOR BOYACK

Illustrated by Elijah Stanfield

Ethan and Emily Tuttle weren't just twins—they were good friends. Sitting together on the bus to their first summer camp, they whistled a camp tune their bus driver, Donald, had taught them.

"We're here!" Emily shouted excitedly as the camp came into view.

As the bus drove into the camp, the children could see all the exciting activities they would be doing—swimming in the lake, archery, an obstacle course, and more.

"Hey, it's Mrs. Miner!" Ethan shouted as the bus came to a stop, pointing to their favorite teacher from school. They were happy to see a familiar face.

"It's the Tuttle twins!" she said with a smile. "I'm so glad to see the two of you. Mr. Miner and I will be helping Chief Ron this summer as camp counselors."

The children unloaded their bags from the bus and were led by the counselors to four cabins. The Eagle and Turtle cabins were for the boys, and the Bear and Rattlesnake cabins were for the girls.

"Looks like you'll be an Eagle," Emily remarked to Ethan, seeing his blue handkerchief. "I get to be a

Rattlesnake," she added, making a loud hissing sound to tease her brother.

"Much of your camp experience this week will be a series of competitions," Mr. Miner told all the children. "Your cabinmates are also your teammates; we hope everyone will try their best!"

"Chief Ron will present the winner of each activity with a special ribbon to attach to their team flag," Mrs. Miner said, "in recognition of their good performance and teamwork."

"The Eagles are going to win, obviously," Ethan said. "We're a fearsome predator!"

"Yeah, you're going down!" added Julian, another Eagle, pointing to the other teams.

"Better be careful..." Emily calmly replied. "You know that rattlesnakes sometimes bite if they are threatened," she said, smiling slyly.

"That's right... watch out, Eagles!" warned another Rattlesnake named Charlotte.

The twins each went to their cabins and spent the rest of the afternoon getting to know their new teammates.

Ethan and Emily liked the kids on their teams and had no trouble making friends with everyone. Summer camp was going to be awesome!

One of Emily's new friends, Kate, was a bit worried about Julian. "He makes me nervous and sort of seems like a bully," she said. "We need to be careful in case he tries anything."

Meanwhile, the Eagles were trying to figure out how they could win the camp competition.

"If the rest of them are anything like my sister, I think the Rattlesnakes might be tough to beat," Ethan said.

"Don't worry about that," Julian quickly replied. "I've got an idea..."

The first competition came the next morning after breakfast—a canoe race at the lake.

When Mr. Miner shouted "GO!" all the teams began paddling furiously toward the opposite shore. The Rattlesnakes got off to an early start, but got tired quickly and slowed down. The Eagles edged past them and the other teams, winning the race.

As Chief Ron attached a ribbon to the Eagles' flag, Ethan helped Emily pull the Rattlesnakes' canoe onto the sand, and discovered that a very large rock had been tied to the back, weighing them down during the race.

Ethan shot a glance at Julian, who was giggling to himself. "Shhh," he whispered to Ethan.

Over the next couple of days, nothing seemed to go right for the Rattlesnakes—bent arrows, wet firewood, muddy ground, and more.

Seeing the Eagles smirk and whisper each time they won made Emily suspicious that her team's bad luck was not an accident.

The Rattlesnakes were upset, feeling like they had been unfairly targeted. During one of their meals, the girls plotted their *revenge* to get back at the Eagles for what they had done.

"We can't let them get away with this," said Kate. "We need to—"

She was interrupted by the Eagles, who began loudly singing their team chant.

Soaring in the sky above,
Our mighty wings we show.
Hunting all the others,
Who are our prey below.

Ethan was getting into the team spirit, and certainly liked being part of the winning team!

"Oh, so we're prey now?" Emily said in disgust. "It's time to teach these guys a lesson."

That afternoon, the counselors led the children to
the large obstacle course for their next activity.
There were all sorts of challenges: tunnels, climbing
walls, rope swings, and more. Emily clapped her
hands in anticipation!

"To win, your entire team must cross the finish line
without falling," Mr. Miner told them. The children
dashed onto the course as he shouted "GO!"

After Charlotte hopped off the rope swing, she
moved the landing platform, making Julian fall into
the mud so he had to start over.

Emily began to giggle, getting excited that they were in the lead. As she approached the balance beams, she decided to help her team as well.

"Look out!" she shouted to Ethan, who was working his way along the beam next to her. He turned his head, lost his balance, and fell into the mud pit below.

"Ugh, no fair!" he shouted in frustration.

The Rattlesnakes' revenge seemed to pay off—they won a ribbon for their team flag!

Late that night, the Rattlesnakes crept into the Eagles' cabin and set up all kinds of pranks that Kate had thought up. The boys were fast asleep and didn't notice a thing.

"These boys are in for a big surprise," Emily thought to herself. "This will teach them for messing with the Rattlesnakes!"

The Eagles awoke the next morning to discover they had been pranked—toilet paper was thrown around and itchy wood chips were in their blankets.

As Julian got out of bed, he startled the skunk that had been sleeping underneath.

"Ahhh!" the kids shouted as the scared skunk let out a foul spray, running towards the door.

The boys tried to wash up, but discovered someone had put dye in the water tank, which turned Emmett's skin blue.

Suddenly a scream came from the bathroom— Ethan ran out, startled by a snake.

"This means war!" Julian said, coughing from the stench. "We have to get even..." he said, clenching his fists.

The Eagles missed breakfast and were late for the morning meeting at the center of camp. The other teams stood as far away as they could, plugging their noses. Apparently the skunk smell hadn't washed off of Julian and his teammates as much as they thought...

"Today's activity will be an orienteering race,"
Mr. Miner announced to the children. Most didn't
know what orienteering was, so he explained that
it involves using a compass to figure out what
direction you should travel. "Each team will follow a
different path lined with team markers," he said.

"At these points you will need to solve a math problem," Mrs. Miner explained. "Once solved, it will reveal what direction you must travel to find the next marker and a new clue. Keep solving the problems until you reach the end."

Chief Ron rang a bell to signal the start of the race. The children huddled around their different team markers and opened their first clues.

Ethan loved doing math. He helped his team quickly solve the problem. The Eagles used their compass to proceed in a straight line at 74 degrees west, putting them in first place right at the beginning.

"Let's go!" Julian shouted to his teammates as he ran into the woods. "That ribbon is ours!"

The Eagles soon found other markers and solved those problems just as fast as the first. Ethan was proud that his math skills were being put to use.

The clues pointed them down a path that led behind a waterfall. Inside a shallow cave was a small version of the camp totem pole. "This must be where all the teams' paths will lead," Ethan guessed.

Attached was the final clue, and Julian read it to the group. "Though we all walk different paths in life, we still walk together as one," the note read. "Solve the following problem to learn which direction you should all follow."

The Eagles did the math and Ethan led the group, with the compass pointing the way.

"Wait up, guys!" Julian shouted from behind.

"What were you doing back there?" Ethan asked him, curious why he had fallen behind.

"You want to keep winning, right?" Julian asked. "I did what I had to do." Ethan could hear the other groups catching up behind them.

The Eagles arrived in a meadow where the counselors were waiting on horses. When the Eagles realized they had won, they began chanting:

Soaring in the sky above,
Our mighty wings we show.
Hunting all the others,
Who are our prey below.

Chief Ron added a green ribbon to their already impressive collection.

"How did we get so far ahead?" Ethan wondered out loud. "The others aren't behind us anymore."

"I changed the numbers on the final clue so the others would go in the wrong direction," Julian quietly said to his teammates with a devilish grin.

"That's not very nice," Emmett reluctantly protested. "Ethan was helping us win without cheating. I think it's more fun to win when we do it the right way."

"The other teams should have gotten here by now," Mrs. Miner said, looking at her watch.

Ethan saw how nervous she was becoming, which made him feel bad about what his team had done. He was worried about his sister and what might happen if all the other kids were really lost.

"Mrs. Miner," Ethan said, "I think the other teams might need help. The numbers on the last clue were changed... they went in the wrong direction."

Mrs. Miner told the other adults, and they all set off on horseback to bring the children back safely.

It took a while, but the counselors found the other teams and helped the group get back to camp. Nobody was hurt, but they were very, *very* grumpy. Ethan was glad Emily was alright.

Chief Ron emerged from his cabin. "Gather everyone after the sun sets," he said to the other counselors. "It's time for a lesson."

He was wearing a feathered headdress, traditional clothing, and looked very wise. "That must be why he's called 'The Chief,'" Emily said.

That night, all of the children took a seat near the fire, not knowing what to expect. The sound of drums filled the air as Mr. and Mrs. Miner, dressed as Native Americans, danced around the fire.

"These warriors represent the conflicts of people throughout history," the chief announced. "We are all part of the human family, brothers and sisters, and yet sometimes we live in fear of people

who are from different tribes and nations. We fight, when we could be friends."

The warriors began pretending to fight with one another. Ethan and Emily liked the dancing but were unsure why the counselors were doing this.

"Your teams are like tribes, and rather than being friends, you have fought," he said. "*Why?*" he asked the group.

"I didn't like being picked on," Kate responded.

"We didn't want to lose," Julian added.

"I got jealous when other teams were winning," Ethan said.

Chief Ron nodded slowly. "You have acted based on fear," he said. "Fear *can* be a good thing, because it drives us to act when real danger is upon us or when we need to defend ourselves."

Mrs. Miner lifted a hatchet to pretend to attack Mr. Miner, who immediately defended himself with a shield. This made the kids giggle.

"But fear can also drive us to attack others—as you all have done! It is wrong to use force against another person or their property," the chief explained. "It is okay to defend yourself if attacked, but you must never become the attacker. It is wrong to be the aggressor."

REVENGE

BLOWBACK

REVENGE

"But Chief, the Eagles cheated first... it wasn't fair, so we had to make it even," Emily said.

"*Justice* is when balance is restored—when a wrong is made right. But revenge is not justice," Ron explained. "Revenge just adds another wrong."

As he spoke, the golden ring behind him burst into flames and the drums grew louder. The two warriors began dancing again, pretending to fight back and forth.

"An act of revenge invites *blowback*—another attack from those who were attacked," Chief Ron said. He looked at each team. "And this cycle of revenge could continue, back and forth, forever. You have seen this in yourselves, have you not?"

The children all nodded. Ethan realized that picking on the other teams caused blowback.

Emily had thought getting revenge would make the Eagles stop cheating, but it actually made them fight back even harder.

"You must stop the cycle of revenge and walk a better path in life," the chief continued. "Calm the fear in your enemy. This is the only way to begin a new cycle of peace and prosperity."

The drums and the warriors stopped as Chief Ron interpreted symbols from a parchment. "Do not hurt your neighbor, for it is not him that you hurt, but rather yourself. Instead," he added, "do good to your neighbor, adding to his days of happiness as you add to your own."

Emily leaned over to Ethan to whisper in his ear. "That's sort of like what Mom and Dad say: 'Treat others the way you want to be treated.'"

"This can be explained another way, my young friends. It is often known as the *Golden Rule*," the chief explained. "My people believe in this rule, but it is not only ours. It is common wisdom in many cultures and religions."

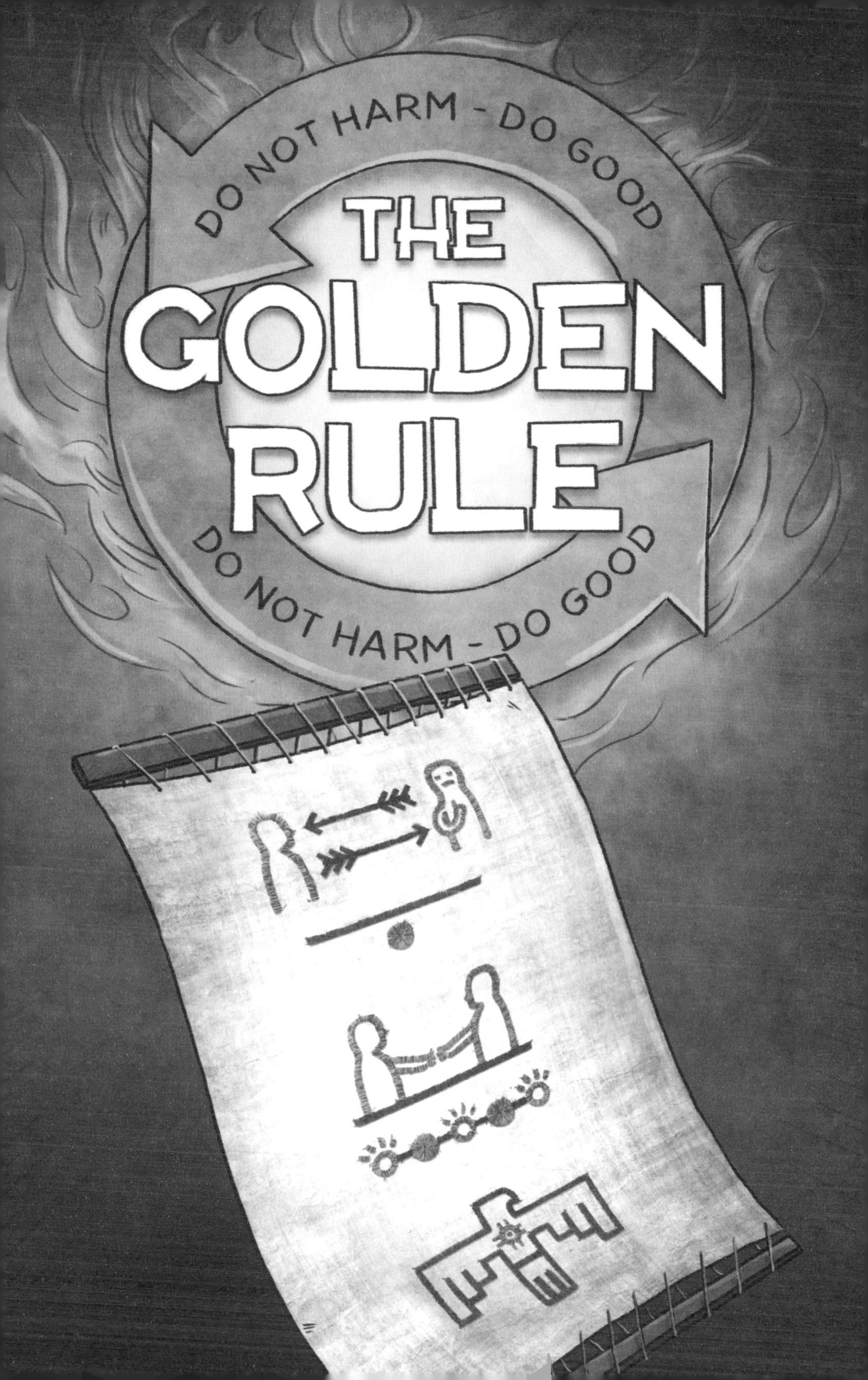
DO NOT HARM - DO GOOD
THE GOLDEN RULE
DO NOT HARM - DO GOOD

Mr. and Mrs. Miner jumped forward with their weapons. "Do any of you enjoy being attacked?" Mr. Miner asked.

Wide-eyed and startled, the children all responded together, "No!"

"Then you, yourself, must choose to live by the *principle of non-aggression*—to never attack another person or their belongings, and only use force to defend yourself," Chief Ron said. "Only then can you live in lasting peace with others."

The warriors dropped their weapons. "Would you prefer to be treated with kindness?" Mrs. Miner asked the children.

They all smiled and shouted together, "Yes!"

"Then you, yourself, must choose to treat others with kindness and respect," Chief Ron said. "Only then can we enjoy prosperity in our lives."

Smoke erupted as the chief threw something into the fire. When the smoke faded, the warriors had disappeared.

Chief Ron concluded, "Ending the cycle of revenge is the most difficult step. It requires each of you to let go of fear, forgive the other person, and bravely extend an arm of friendship."

"I'm sorry for causing problems, Emily," Ethan said. "Me, too," she replied. The twins hugged as kids from different teams shook hands and apologized.

"I challenge each of you to live the Golden Rule for the remainder of the week," Chief Ron said.

The teams returned to their cabins, thinking about all the things they had learned.

It rained all that night, but in the morning it was clear enough for a day hike. Each team carried their flag as they climbed up a nearby mountain.

"On a team you have a common identity and can work together to accomplish more than what you could alone," the chief explained as they began. "Our differences are valuable. If everyone was the same, we couldn't help or learn from one another."

When they reached the top later that morning, the children ate lunch while enjoying the view.

"Being different from one another, or being on different teams, should not divide us," Mrs. Miner said. "It should bring us closer together."

She and Mr. Miner then gave a special friendship bracelet to each child to remind them of the lesson they learned from the chief.

"Look, it's golden," Emily pointed out to the others. "Just like the Golden Rule!"

A flash of lightning appeared in the distance, followed by a loud clap of thunder. KABOOM! The group began their trek down the mountain, getting soaked in the heavy downpour of rain.

"The camp is flooding!" Emily shouted as they approached the cabins. The storms had caused the nearby river to begin overflowing, and water was running into the campground.

"This week you have fought," Chief Ron said. "Now you have an opportunity to *collaborate*—to work together on something important. We must divert the water to protect the camp!"

Each team took a different task and got to work. The Bears and Turtles worked together filling sandbags. Shoveling over and over was hard work!

The Rattlesnakes and Eagles formed a human chain to move each sandbag to the water's edge and stack them to build a wall. The counselors helped here and there, and made sure everybody was safe.

"They need some extra help," Mrs. Miner said, seeing the children struggle. She began walking towards them to lend a hand.

"No," Ron replied. "What they need is this experience of working together to solve a problem. Let's let them do the work, and enjoy the benefit."

When the children had finished, they were tired, hungry, and covered in mud. But they had achieved their goal!

The group watched as pools of water came close to the camp, but were stopped by the wall of sandbags. "We did it!" many of them exclaimed, giving high fives to one another.

"Wait until our parents hear about this!" Ethan remarked to some of his friends from other teams.

"That was hard work, but I actually had fun doing it!" Charlotte replied.

"Do you see what happened?" Chief Ron asked the children. They shook their heads, confused. "Look at yourselves right now—you're not divided by teams, and you're not fighting. This experience brought you together to work on something bigger than yourselves or your individual teams."

Everybody gathered together in the dining lodge to dry off and talk about their latest adventure.

Mrs. Miner joined them with an armful of ingredients to make S'mores. "We're very proud of each of you," she said. "And now that you've applied the Golden Rule, how about we golden up some of these marshmallows?" she said with a wink.

As Emily ran to grab a marshmallow, she stopped short, remembering to treat others the way she would want to be treated.

"After you," she said to Julian, who was right behind her. Ethan, watching from beside the fireplace, gave her a thumbs up.

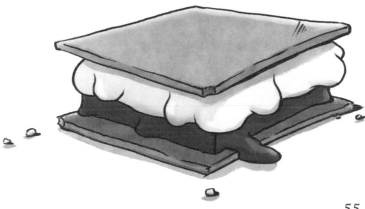

The final days of summer camp were much more enjoyable than how it started. Ethan loved spending time at the archery range and Emily learned how to make Native American jewelry.

Even though the teams still competed against one another in some of the activities, they did so fairly, and more importantly focused on doing their best, having fun, and treating everybody nicely.

Chief Ron watched the children as they carried their bags to the bus on the last day of camp. "Don't fear others—be friends!" he shouted. "And don't forget the Golden Rule!" he shouted, waving goodbye.

"We won't!" the Tuttle twins and their new friends shouted back, holding up their new golden bracelets—a constant reminder to always treat others the way that they want others to treat them.

The End

Hi, parents!
I'm Ron Paul.

As a congressman from Texas, I spent many years encouraging my colleagues to treat other countries and people the way we would want them to treat us.

Many of my speeches were compiled into a book, *A Foreign Policy of Freedom*. In it, I discuss the same principles your family read about in this fun book: peace, friendship, the Golden Rule, and the non-aggression principle.

These ideas apply as much to international relations between governments as they do to our family relationships. That's the wonderful thing about fundamental principles—they apply to all people in all circumstances. Wherever you are from, and whatever your life is like, you can choose to put the Golden Rule into practice.

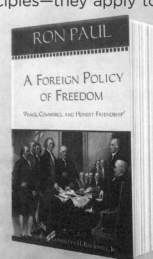

Make sure to share these principles with your friends—our success in adopting them will determine whether or not we will enjoy peace and prosperity in the generations to come.

The Author

Connor Boyack is president of Libertas Institute, a free market think tank in Utah. In that capacity he has changed a significant number of laws in favor of personal freedom and free markets, and has launched a variety of educational projects, including The Tuttle Twins children's book series. Connor is the author of over a dozen books.

A California native and Brigham Young University graduate, Connor currently resides in Lehi, Utah, with his wife and two children.

The Illustrator

Elijah Stanfield is owner of Red House Motion Imaging, a media production company in Washington.

A longtime student of Austrian economics, history, and the classical liberal philosophy, Elijah has dedicated much of his time and energy to promoting the ideas of free markets and individual liberty. Some of his more notable works include producing eight videos in support of Ron Paul's 2012 presidential candidacy. He currently resides in Richland, Washington, with his wife April and their six children.

Contact us at TuttleTwins.com!

Glossary of Terms

Blowback: The negative, unintended consequences of harming or interfering with others.

Collaborate: To work together with others on an activity, especially to produce or create something.

Golden Rule: A general principle holding that a person should treat others the way that the person wishes to be treated by them.

Justice: A morally correct outcome that is fair and reasonable.

Non-Aggression Principle: A general principle holding that one should never use violence against another person, except only in defense against another's aggression.

Revenge: Hurting another person because they first hurt you.

Discussion Questions

1. Why is it wrong to be an aggressor, causing harm or fear in another person?
2. In what cases is it justified to fight another person, if any?
3. Why is adhering to the Golden Rule difficult?
4. What would the world look like if warring nations followed the principle of non-aggression?
5. How can you more closely follow the Golden Rule in your life?

Don't Forget the Activity Workbook!

Visit **TuttleTwins.com/GoldenWorkbook** to download the PDF and provide your children with all sorts of activities to reinforce the lessons they learned in the book!